Ingredients for a Healthy Life

DELICIOUS DAIRY Recipes

Gareth Stevens
PUBLISHING

By Kristen Rajczak

Please visit our website, www.garethstevens.com. For a free color catalog of all our high-quality books, call toll free 1-800-542-2595 or fax 1-877-542-2596.

Library of Congress Cataloging-in-Publication Data

Rajczak, Kristen.
Delicious dairy recipes / by Kristen Rajczak.
  p. cm. — (Ingredients for a healthy life)
Includes index.
ISBN 978-1-4824-0562-0 (pbk.)
ISBN 978-1-4824-0564-4 (6-pack)
ISBN 978-1-4824-0561-3 (library binding)
1. Cooking (Dairy products) — Juvenile literature. I. Rajczak, Kristen. II. Title.
TX759.R35 2014
641.3—dc23

First Edition

Published in 2015 by
Gareth Stevens Publishing
111 East 14th Street, Suite 349
New York, NY 10003

Copyright © 2015 Gareth Stevens Publishing

Designer: Andrea Davison-Bartolotta
Editor: Kristen Rajczak

Photo credits: Cover, back cover, pp. 1, 3, 9, 11, 13, 15, 19, 21–24 (milk bottle background) schwarzhana/Shutterstock.com; cover, p. 1 (vegetable and dip) bernashafo/Shutterstock.com; cover, pp. 1 (milkshake, cheesecake), 13, 14, 21 (arrows) iStockphoto/Thinkstock; p. 4 mexrix/Shutterstock.com; p. 5 Fuse/Getty Images; p. 6 Khvost/Shutterstock.com; p. 7 English School/The Bridgeman Art Library/Getty Images; p. 9 (milkshake) Carlos Restrepo/Shutterstock.com; p. 9 (bananas) digitalvox/Shutterstock.com; p. 9 (strawberries) Aleksey Troshin/Shutterstock.com; p. 9 (blueberries) ravi/Shutterstock.com; p. 10 Cameron Davidson/Workbook Stock/Getty Images; p. 11 (ice cream) Olga Lyubkina/Shutterstock.com; p. 11 (almonds) Roxana Bashyrova/Shutterstock.com; p. 11 (hot fudge) Marie C Fields/Shutterstock.com; p. 11 (marshmallows) Matt Antonino/Shutterstock.com; p. 12 Creatas/Thinkstock; p 15 David P. Smith/Shutterstock.com; p. 16 Shah Rohani/Shutterstock.com; p. 17 Image Source/Getty Images; p. 19 Innershadows/iStock.Thinkstock; p. 20 Robyn Mackenzie/Shutterstock.com; p. 21 (boy) Monkey Business/Thinkstock.

Printed in the United States of America

CPSIA compliance information: Batch #CS15GS: For further information contact Gareth Stevens, New York, New York at 1-800-542-2595.

Contents

!
Recipes in this book may use knives, mixers, and hot stove tops. Ask for an adult's help when using these tools.

Words in the glossary appear in **bold** type the first time they are used in the text.

All About Dairy

Do you scream for ice cream? Does cheddar make everything better? If you answered yes, you must be a dairy lover! Dairy is a food group that includes all kinds of milk products. From the Parmesan cheese on spaghetti to the sour cream on top of a taco, there are so many delicious meals that include dairy!

Dairy products have health benefits, too. Read on to find out the great things dairy can do for your body—and your taste buds!

Do You Have Allergies?

The **recipes** in this book may use **ingredients** that contain or have come into contact with nuts, gluten, dairy products, and other common causes of **allergies**. If you have any food allergies, please ask a parent or teacher for help when cooking and tasting!

Drinking a glass of milk is an easy way to get the health benefits of dairy.

In Human History

Milk is the basis of all dairy products, and has been part of the human **diet** for more than 10,000 years. People began to use milk as food around the time they began living in communities and raising animals for food.

By the time explorers were heading to the Americas, cow's milk was common in Europe. European dairy cows were brought to North America during the early 1600s. By the late 1800s, milkmen were delivering milk to people's homes in glass bottles.

CHEW ON THIS!

While cow's milk is the most popular milk in the United States, other animals' milk is used around the world, including milk from goats, buffalo, sheep, and reindeer.

dairy cows

In ancient Egypt, milk was only served to kings and queens, or those who had a lot of money.

What's in It?

Milk is part water and contains fats, protein, and carbohydrates, three of the main groups of **nutrients** our body needs. Fat is one of the body's major building blocks. Some people don't want to take in too much fat, so dairy companies have found ways to take some of it out of milk.

Common types of milk include:

- **whole milk**: about 4 percent milk fat, none has been removed
- **2 percent milk**: 2 percent milk fat, about half has been removed
- **1 percent milk**: 1 percent milk fat, contains half as much as 2 percent milk
- **skim milk**: has almost all milk fat removed

CHEW ON THIS!

Fat can be broken down and used as energy or stored for later use. Dairy is a good source of healthy fats, such as those used to build up your brain and **cells**. The unhealthy fats contained in some dairy products are discussed later in this book.

Chocolate Banana Milkshake

makes 2 big milkshakes or 4 small servings

Ingredients:

2 large, ripe bananas
1 1/2 cups skim milk
1/4 cup low-fat vanilla yogurt
2 tablespoons cocoa powder
1 teaspoon vanilla extract
ice (about two handfuls, or 8 cubes)

Directions:

1. Cut the bananas into a few smaller pieces. Put into a blender with the cocoa powder, yogurt, vanilla, and milk.
2. Blend together.
3. Add the ice to the blender. Blend until smooth.

This healthy milkshake can be customized! Not a banana lover? Use strawberries or blueberries! However you mix it up, this milkshake will give you a delicious helping of dairy.

Milk Processing

Fat removal is just one part of milk **processing**. In 1862, Louis Pasteur began heating milk to high temperatures to kill any harmful **bacteria**. By 1895, this practice—called pasteurization—had become standard in dairy companies.

Homogenization is another way milk is processed, especially in the United States. High pressure and heat are used to break up the fat in milk so all parts of it are well mixed. Homogenization is especially important for milk being used to make ice cream!

CHEW ON THIS!

Before homogenization, the fat in milk floated to the top as cream. People would either shake up the bottle of milk to blend it in or skim it off the top.

milk bottling plant

Fudgey S'more Ice Cream Cake

makes about 9 servings

Ingredients:

Crust:

about 8 ounces of graham crackers

1 cup whole almonds, toasted

3 tablespoons sugar

1/2 cup (1 stick) light, unsalted butter, melted

Filling:

1 1/2 quarts low-fat chocolate ice cream, softened until spreadable

1 cup hot fudge from a jar (not heated)

1 cup marshmallow crème from a jar

2 cups miniature marshmallows

Directions:

1. Preheat oven to 350 degrees.
2. Use a food processor or high-powered blender to grind graham crackers, toasted almonds, and sugar. Add melted butter and mix until moist crumbs form.
3. Press crust mixture into the bottom and up the sides of a 9 x 9 pan. Bake about 12 minutes. Allow crust to cool.
4. Spread about half the softened ice cream into the crust. Spoon half of the hot fudge over the top. Freeze until the fudge is set, about 10 minutes.
5. Repeat with the rest of the ice cream and hot fudge. Cover and freeze the cake for several hours or overnight.
6. When the cake is frozen, preheat the oven's broiler.
7. Spread marshmallow crème over top of cake. Sprinkle miniature marshmallows over in single layer. Broil for about 1 minute, just until marshmallows are deep brown.
8. Serve cake immediately with warmed hot fudge!

This dessert showcases ice cream as a tasty dairy product. Ask an adult for help using the food processor and oven.

Adding a Little Culture

Some of the most useful and popular dairy products are cultured, or made by adding certain bacteria to milk and letting them grow. The flavors of buttermilk, sour cream, and yogurt all come from this **fermentation** process.

Yogurt has been around for centuries in diets around the world, including countries in eastern Europe and western Asia. Today, scientists have discovered lots of health benefits. Cultured dairy products, such as yogurt, help keep up the populations of good bacteria living in our bodies.

CHEW ON THIS!

Here's an easy, healthy way to enjoy protein-packed yogurt! Choose your favorite low-fat yogurt and spoon some into a tall glass. Add a layer of nuts or granola and a layer of fruit, such as sliced strawberries. Repeat the layers two more times. Now you have a great yogurt parfait (pahr-FAY)!

Yummy Yogurt Dip

Ingredients:

1 6-ounce container of plain, low-fat yogurt
1 garlic clove, minced
2 tablespoons chopped chives
1/4 teaspoon salt
1/4 teaspoon pepper
1/4 teaspoon dried dill
1 tablespoon lemon juice
vegetable dippers

Yogurt can be used to make so many different dips. Here's one easy recipe that gives you all the health benefits of yogurt and a dose of your favorite tasty veggies.

Directions:

1. Chop garlic clove and chives.
2. Mix all ingredients together. Refrigerate until it's served.
3. Slice the vegetables you want to dip with, such as carrots, bell peppers, cucumbers, broccoli, celery, or cherry tomatoes. Pita chips would taste great, too!

Cheese, Please!

Cheese is another cultured dairy product. It's commonly thought that the first cheese was made in the Middle East. Ancient Greeks and Romans ate cheese, and it was part of the Pilgrims' stores aboard the *Mayflower* as they traveled from England to North America.

In 2011, more than 2 billion pounds of cheese were sold in the United States alone! It's no wonder—from mozzarella on pizza to a slice of cheddar on a sandwich, there are so many uses for the many tasty types of cheese.

CHEW ON THIS!

Since cheese is a food that's high in **calories**, it should be just a small part of what you eat. Low-fat cheeses, as with yogurts and other dairy products, are a smart choice for a balanced diet.

Whole-Wheat Buttermilk Cheddar Biscuits

makes 8 to 10 biscuits

Ingredients:

2 cups whole-wheat flour
4 teaspoons baking powder
1/2 teaspoon salt
1/4 cup (1/2 stick) unsalted, light butter, chilled
3/4 cup low-fat cheddar cheese, grated
1 cup buttermilk

These biscuits use butter, cheese, and buttermilk—all great dairy ingredients. They're also made with whole-wheat flour, which is a healthier choice than white flour when baking.

Directions:

1. Preheat the oven to 450 degrees.
2. Measure flour, baking powder, and salt into a medium-sized bowl. Mix together with a fork.
3. Cut the 1/2 stick of cold butter into little pea-sized pieces. Add to the flour mixture. With a fork or your hands, mash the butter pieces into the flour so it looks like crumbs.
4. Stir in the grated cheese.
5. Pour in the buttermilk. Mix together until it's just combined. **Knead** the dough with your hands 8 to 10 times.
6. Sprinkle a little flour on your countertop. Turn the biscuit dough onto the floured surface and press it flat until it's about 3/4 inch thick.
7. Use a drinking glass to cut out biscuit rounds, or use cookie cutters to make fun shapes!
8. Put the rounds on an ungreased baking sheet and bake 10 to 12 minutes or until lightly browned.

Good for You

Eating dairy products can be delicious and good for your body. You already read how healthy fats help cells grow and repair, but the protein in dairy products also does this in muscles.

Dairy products are good sources of vitamins and minerals, which are two other kinds of nutrients that make your body work well. The B vitamins found in milk give you healthier skin and blood. The calcium in milk makes your bones stronger. Potassium and magnesium are other important minerals you can get from milk.

CHEW ON THIS!

Pasteurization destroys some of the vitamins found in milk. In the United States, some milk and dairy products are fortified with vitamins A and D, which means they've had these vitamins added back into them.

Nutrition Facts
Serving Size 1 cup (240 mL)
Servings Per Container about 8

Amount Per Serving

Calories 110   Calories from Fat 20

	% Daily Value
Total Fat 2.5g	4%
Saturated Fat 1.5g	8%
Trans Fat 0g	
Cholesterol 15mg	4%
Sodium 130mg	5%
Total Carbohydrate 13g	4%
Dietary Fiber 0g	0%
Sugars 12g	
Protein 9g	18%

Vitamin A 10% • Vitamin C 4%
Calcium 30% • Iron 0% • Vitamin D 25%

Percent Daily Values are based on a 2,000 calorie diet. Your daily values may be higher or lower depending on your calorie needs.

	Calories:	2,000	2,500
Total Fat	Less than	65g	80g
Sat Fat	Less than	20g	25g
Cholesterol	Less than	300mg	300mg
Sodium	Less than	2,400mg	2,400mg
Total Carbohydrate		300g	375g
Dietary Fiber		25g	30g
Protein		50g	65g

Calories per gram: Fat 9 • Carbohydrate 4 • Protein 4

Amounts Per Cup Serving	Fat
	%
Whole Milk	
Lowfat Milk	1.5

Buying milk can be a healthy choice for your whole family.

Not Too Much

Doctors and scientists warn against eating too much saturated fat. It raises the level of cholesterol in your blood. Cholesterol is a waxy substance your body needs to build cells and do other activities. But if too much builds up in the body, cholesterol can lead to many health problems, such as heart disease.

Whole-fat dairy products, such as cheese and ice cream, can contain more saturated fat than you need. It's OK to eat these foods in small amounts. That's why the cheesecakes on the next page are just cupcake size!

CHEW ON THIS!

Some people are lactose intolerant, or unable to break down lactose, the main carbohydrate in milk products. Drinking milk or eating ice cream can give them cramps, stomachaches, and worse.

Mini Cheesecakes

makes 6 cupcake-sized cheesecakes

Ingredients:

Crust:
1/3 cup graham cracker crumbs
1 tablespoon white sugar
1 tablespoon light butter

Filling:
1 8-ounce package low-fat cream cheese, softened
1/4 cup white sugar
1 1/2 teaspoons lemon juice
1/4 teaspoon vanilla extract
1 egg

Low-fat cream cheese and light butter make this a healthier dessert to share with your family and friends. You can also add fruit on top!

Directions:

1. Preheat oven to 325 degrees. Lightly grease a 6-cup muffin pan. You can also use cupcake liners instead.
2. In a medium bowl, microwave your butter on high for about 15 seconds. Mix in the graham cracker crumbs and sugar. Spoon some of the mixture into the muffin cups until each has about the same amount. Press into the bottom of the cup firmly.
3. Bake the crusts for 5 minutes, then remove them to cool. Keep the oven on.
4. Use a microwave-safe bowl to soften the cream cheese, setting the microwave on high for about 30 seconds.
5. Use a mixer to beat together the softened cream cheese, sugar, lemon juice, and vanilla until fluffy.
6. Mix in the egg.
7. Pour the cream cheese mixture into the muffin cups until each is about 3/4 full. Bake for 25 minutes.
8. Allow the mini cheesecakes to cool. Keep them in the refrigerator until you're ready to eat them!

19

Healthy Choices

Here are some more ideas on how to include dairy in a healthy diet:

- Replace butter or oil in a recipe with the same amount of low-fat, plain yogurt to cut down fat and add some protein to your baked goods.

- Add fruit to yogurt instead of buying the flavored kinds. Try cool combinations like mango and blueberry!

- Make your own pizza with a frozen, whole-wheat crust, and slices of fresh mozzarella and tomatoes.

- Drink low-fat milk instead of a soda with your meals.

Healthy Reasons to Eat Dairy

Calcium, phosphorus, and vitamin D aid in bone growth and strength.

Protein helps build and repair muscle.

Cultured dairy products benefit the good bacteria in the body.

Carbohydrates in milk are broken down and used for energy.

Glossary

allergy: a body's sensitivity to usually harmless things in the surroundings, such as dust, pollen, or mold

bacteria: tiny creatures that can only be seen with a microscope. Some can cause illness, while others are helpful.

calorie: a unit of energy in food

cell: the smallest basic part of a living thing

diet: the food one usually eats

fermentation: a process by which an organism changes a sugar or starch into an alcohol or acid in the absence of oxygen

ingredient: a food that is mixed with other foods

knead: to work with dough until it's smooth

nutrient: something a living thing needs to grow and stay alive

processing: subjecting to a special treatment

recipe: an explanation of how to make food

For More Information

BOOKS

Dambra, Marianne E. *Cooking Is Cool: Heat-Free Recipes for Kids to Cook.* St. Paul, MN: Redleaf Press, 2013.

Parker, Vic. *All About Dairy.* Irvine, CA: QEB Publishing, 2009.

WEBSITES

The Dairy Connection: Recipes
www.nationaldairycouncil.org/recipes/Pages/RecipeLanding.aspx
Find creative ways to use dairy in your meals every day.

Dairy Fun Facts
www.southwestdairyfarmers.com/fun_facts
Learn more about where dairy products come from, and search for your next recipe!

The Story of Milk
www.moomilk.com/virtual-tour
Follow this link to see how milk travels from a cow to your table.

Index